WM. TYRRELL & CO.
TORONTO

Little Jeanne of France

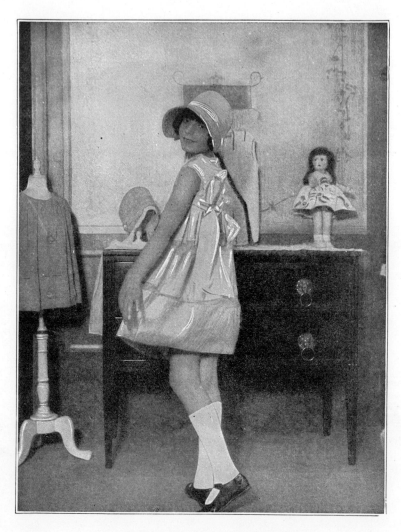

LITTLE JEANNE OF FRANCE

LITTLE JEANNE
of FRANCE

BY

MADELINE BRANDEIS

Producer of the Motion Pictures

"The Little Indian Weaver"
"The Wee Scotch Piper"
"The Little Dutch Tulip Girl"
"The Little Swiss Wood Carver"

Distributed by Pathé Exchange, Inc., New York City

Photographic Illustrations made in France by the Author

GROSSET & DUNLAP
PUBLISHERS   NEW YORK
by arrangement with the A. Flanagan Company

PREFACE

When I began to write these stories about children of all lands I had just returned from Europe whither I journeyed with Marie and Ref. Maybe you don't know Marie and Ref. I'll introduce them: Please meet Marie, my very little daughter, and Ref, my very big reflex camera.

These two are my helpers. Marie helps by being a little girl who knows what other little girls like and by telling me; and Ref helps by snapping pictures of everything interesting that Marie and I see on our travels. I couldn't get along without them.

Several years have gone by since we started our work together and Marie is a bigger girl—but Ref hasn't changed one bit. Ref hasn't changed any more than my interest in writing these books for you. And I hope that *you* hope that I'll never change, because I want to keep on writing until we'll have no more countries to write about—unless, of course, some one discovers a new country.

Even if a new country isn't discovered, we'll find foreign children to talk about—maybe the children

in Mars! Who knows? Nobody. Not even Marie—
and Marie usually knows about most things. That's
the reason why, you see, though I sign myself

Madeline Brandeis

I am really only

Marie's Mother.

DEDICATION

To every child of every land,
    Little sister, little brother,
As in this book your lives unfold,
    May you learn to love each other.

CONTENTS

THE BOIS DE BOULOGNE (Page 90)

Little Jeanne of France

CHAPTER I

MADAME VILLARD

"The baby is a dear little dark-haired girl, Madame Villard (vē-lär′)," said the nurse.

Madame Villard came forward, and her face expressed the joy in her heart.

It was the twilight hour. Paris was busily honking and tooting outside the broad windows of Madame Villard's apartment.

The apartment looked out upon one of Paris' finest avenues. And Paris has many fine avenues. This had been Madame Villard's home for many years.

It was here she had raised her family —her boy and her girl. It was the same girl whose "dear little, dark-haired baby" had just come into the world.

"May I—may I see her?" asked Madame Villard softly.

The nurse led her into the room, and the grandmother looked with tear-dimmed eyes upon this first grandchild.

Baby Margot (mär'-gō) was Madame's first grandchild. At least, that is what Madame thought. Little did Madame Villard know that at this same moment another grandchild of hers was opening wondering brown eyes upon the same world!

The same world and the same coun-

THE APARTMENT ON AVENUE CHAMPS ELYSEES WHERE
MADAME VILLARD LIVED

try, France! Yet how different was this other grandchild's world from the world of little Margot!

Little soft, comfy Margot in her billowy pink and lace down! Little soft, cuddly Margot, whom Grandmother took into her arms that day! All the while, she did not know about the other grandchild.

That other grandchild did not have soft billowy pink and lace pillows on which to rest her head. That other grandchild did not have a grandmother's loving arms into which she could cuddle down.

That other grandchild—but I must not talk of her. I must talk of Margot. For Margot was all that Grandmother

Villard could talk about or even think of that day.

Her own little daughter's daughter! It was so wonderful to think of Margot's being here. So wonderful for poor Madame Villard, whose only son Paul was fighting at the front in the Great War.

When the war had started, Paul had gone to fight for France. Now it was many months since Madame had heard from her soldier boy.

Soon after Paul had joined the army, he had met and married Jeanne (jēn) in a tiny village of France. Paul had written to his mother in Paris, telling her of his marriage.

"You will love Jeanne," wrote Paul.

A QUAINT STREET IN A LITTLE FRENCH VILLAGE FAR FROM
THE ROAR OF CITIES

"When this war is over, I shall bring her to Paris."

But the war was not over, and Jeanne had never been brought to Paris. Madame Villard did not hear from her boy again.

She did not know that on this happy day, while she held her little grandchild Margot in her arms, Paul's little girl was opening her brown eyes upon a different-looking world.

In a sad, war-stricken, bleak little village far from Paris, this other grandchild was born.

CHAPTER II

PAUL

Jeanne's baby was as beautiful as little Margot, though she did not lie upon lacy pillows in a Paris apartment.

Jeanne held the child tightly in her arms, as she rocked back and forth on a broken chair, and as she rocked she looked out upon the poor, little village street. Jeanne was a troubled young mother.

Paul had been at the front for many weeks now. He did not even know that little Jeanne was born. If only Paul would come back to the village!

There was talk of an invasion. Many

small towns of France were being invaded and burned by the enemy. Would this little town be next?

Each day the villagers asked themselves this question and lived in terror. Many had already started to tramp toward Paris. Many were deserting the village.

But Jeanne could not go. There was little Jeanne now. And even if she could have gone, she would never have left until her Paul had come back.

Each day a letter went to Paul at the front. Each day Jeanne trembled at the postman's footsteps outside her door.

But no news. Only whispers and more whispers of invasion—invasion!

Oh, if Paul would only come back! Jeanne rocked her baby.

The invasion came. It was one of the last invasions before the Great War came to an end. The enemy burned the little town to the ground.

The great march of the refugees had started. The roads to Paris were alive with homeless people — struggling, homeless humanity, with only the hope of reaching Paris alive.

The village—Paul's village—was a desolate place. As the troop of French soldiers returned after the invasion and marched into it, there was not a soul to be seen. Among those marching French soldiers came Paul.

To the scene of his home he ran. Ev-

A GROUP OF TYPICAL THATCH ROOFED HOUSES IN A LITTLE FRENCH VILLAGE

erything — everything was in ruins!
His house! Gone! His wife!

"Jeanne! Jeanne!" Paul's voice was
a shriek.

"Look, my son, in the cellar. Many
of them hid in cellars for days before."
It was a kind-faced old man speaking.

The distracted Paul dashed into the
underground stone cave and called
again, "Jeanne, oh, Jeanne!"

A little sound came from a corner in
the dark, damp cellar. The soldier
stopped suddenly, and his ears became
those of a forest animal, so sharp, so
alert was he.

"My little one! Jeanne!" he called.

He struck a match. His heart nearly
stopped. His Jeanne was not there.

But something moved in the corner—
something small and white.

"A baby!" Paul gasped.

His voice had dropped to a husky
whisper. He lifted the small, white
bundle. It was a baby—a tiny young
baby!

The soldier carried the child out into
the light. The little one touched his
cheek with a pink hand.

"A baby!" breathed Paul, as he held
this bit of humanity close in his arms.
"And my Jeanne! We were to have had
one like this soon."

Then Paul noticed something around
the baby's neck. A small locket had
been tied around her neck with a piece
of faded ribbon.

With trembling fingers, Paul opened
the locket. The soldier brushed his
hand across his eyes, for he could not
believe what he saw. Inside the locket
was his picture!

CHAPTER III

TO THE FRONT!

Paul sat there and rocked the baby —his baby! He sat and rocked little Jeanne, much as his wife had rocked her before that terrible invasion.

Now his wife was gone. Little Jeanne's mother had not been able to escape as had many of the other villagers. She was dead. Weak and undernourished, the poor woman had been unable to withstand hardships and suffering in a cold, damp cellar.

The invasion had killed little Jeanne's mother. Paul alone now remained to care for this helpless mite.

Paul was a troubled, frantic soldier. He would be called back to the front at any moment. What would he do with the baby?

Just then he heard the bugle and the call to arms: "To the front."

A scurrying soldier passed him and called out, "Make haste. To the front!"

Paul could not move. The baby was asleep in his arms. Little, trusting baby—his baby! The soldier dropped his head in the folds of little Jeanne's dress and sobbed.

A slight tap upon his shoulder brought Paul's head erect. Bending over him was the same old man. It was the kind-faced little peasant who had spoken to him at the cellar door.

"Come, my son," he said, "You are a soldier of France! Would that my old body could fight in your place! But it is you who must go. France needs you, my son."

He slowly helped the soldier to his feet, as the baby in his arms slept on.

Paul saw the light of goodness shining out of the old eyes. With a surge of joy in his heart, he held out his child.

"Oh, my friend," he cried, "if you will take my baby, I can go. I can then go and fight for France. But never, never could I leave her alone, even for France! Take her, friend, and guard her with your life."

The old peasant's eyes grew trou-

A TYPICAL HAMLET IN A BEAUTIFUL SECTION OF FRANCE

bled. For he knew not what he, a poverty-stricken, weakened old man might do with an infant, here in this smoldering ruin of a village. But he held out his arms.

"Yes, I shall take care of her," he promised.

"With your life, my friend," repeated Paul. "Here," he added, as he pulled from his pockets handfuls of small coins. "All I have. Take it. Take her to Paris—to my mother. Wait!"

And Paul then wrote a note — a scrawled, jumbled note—to his mother, Madame Villard, in Paris.

"I am telling her you are coming with my baby—with little Jeanne," he said. "Take her to the address I write on this paper. See! I pin it to her little skirt. Hurry, my friend. Take her. Take her. Adieu, adieu, my little Jeanne!"

The last words were heard afar off, as the father of little Jeanne joined his regiment. Then he marched to the front, into the face of a cruel battle.

The old man stood still and watched the soldier disappearing. He and this baby were the only remaining inhabitants in this town.

The rest were marching, marching, on their way to Paris. He, too, must march to Paris.

An old man with a baby!

It was a long way, but he had given his word to a soldier of France. Did this not make of him a soldier, too?

The old body stiffened, and he stood erect. His hand slowly saluted the departing troops. He, too, was a soldier.

He looked at the address which Paul had pinned to the skirt of little Jeanne: Madame Villard, Avenue Champs Elysées (shän'-zā - lē - zā'), Paris.

Paris? Why, yes; he could walk to Paris. He was a soldier! Marching refugees from other villages were constantly passing. The old man joined the peasant procession.

On his lips were the words, "On, on, on to Paris! On, on, on!"

And little Jeanne thought it was a lullaby and slept.

CHAPTER IV

On trudged the old man. In his arms slept little Jeanne. She was as happy as Margot that day. Margot lay among the sweet-smelling cushions of her baby carriage and was rolled along the smooth walks of Paris parks.

But little Jeanne's "carriage" was not so soft, nor did it roll along. Indeed the old man's gait grew more and more jerky with every step. He watched the rest of the refugees passing him by.

There were families with many children. There were men and women carrying mattresses and clothing, pots and pans. There were dogs running along and barking.

They all passed the old man. Each one had another with whom to walk. But the old man walked alone.

It grew very hard—this walking. He rested often, and each time it was harder to rise and to start the walk again. Only his promise to a soldier of France kept his old body going. At last he dropped heavily at the side of the road.

Jeanne was asleep. The thud awoke her. The old man could go no farther.

Jeanne did not cry. She was happy and satisfied. She had been well cared for. When they had passed farms with cows, little Jeanne had been fed.

The old man looked at her and touched the little soft cheek with his horny hand.

"Little one, I am finished," he whispered. "I have tried so hard, but Paris is too far—too far. It is too far to the front."

With that, the old man slept. Jeanne lay in his arms and blew bubbles to the sky. She watched the trees as they swayed back and forth.

"This world is a pleasant place," it would seem the tiny girl was thinking.

For a long time the old man slept. He was awakened by the sound of a clear voice. He looked into the sad face of a young woman in a black

VERY OLD STONE HOUSES IN A LITTLE VILLAGE OF FRANCE

shawl. She was holding Jeanne's two
little hands in her fingers.

"Is this your baby?" she asked.

"No, no, my child. I am taking her to
Paris to—."

He tried to lift himself but fell back
again.

"You are spent. You must not carry
this child any farther. Come; give her
to me," said the woman.

She took little Jeanne in her arms.
The old man's eyes searched her face
to try to fathom it. He tried to find
there what he hoped to see: kindness.
But all he saw was sadness.

Suzanne Moreau (mō-rō′) was one
of the many refugees who had fled
from her invaded village. She was

one of the few in that long line who
marched alone. Suzanne had always
lived alone, as long as she could remember. Her life had been a lonely
one. She had been a dressmaker in the
small town where she had lived.

Everyone there had known her as
Auntie Sue. She was Auntie Sue to
children and grown-ups alike.

The old man tried to fathom Suzanne
as he looked deep into her eyes and
watched her wrap little Jeanne care-
fully in her shawl.

"I am quite alone," she said. "I am
strong and shall make the march easi-
ly. Do not fear."

She gave her hand to the old man and
he kissed it.

"God bless you," he breathed. Then
he reminded her, "Remember: Avenue
Champs Elysées, Madame Villard."

She nodded her head. She smiled at
him and was off.

CHAPTER V

SUZANNE

It was a month since the day when Madame Villard had received two letters. Just a month had passed since the silver-haired lady and her daughter had pored over two such different letters.

One was a scrawl—Paul's. He wrote that his baby was on her way to Paris to her grandmother. It was a dirty, scrawly note, but full of hope to the two who read it.

The next letter, neat and precise, was from the government. Before they opened it, the two women knew: Paul's

little one was now an orphan. For a
month, how that mother and sister
waited!

With Madame Villard lived her
daughter and her daughter's husband.
They were the parents of Baby Margot.

Margot's father had come back from
the war. But though he had returned
to his dear ones, he would never again
be able to walk. He would be an inva-
lid for life. So Margot's mother had
two helpless ones to care for. And one
of those was Margot's father.

Grandmother had taken care of little
Margot from the day of her birth. Star-
ry-eyed Baby Margot was Grandmother Villard's charge — and a joyous

charge to the old lady. But despite the happiness of her Margot, the heart of Madame Villard yearned for that other wee one—her son's little orphaned daughter.

She waited longingly for Paul's child to be brought to her. She waited until she could wait no longer. Then she went out in search of little Jeanne.

Madame Villard traveled to many villages in her search. She even asked the government to help her.

She tried so hard to speed the little one's arrival. But she could not. The child was never brought to her.

And now, to-day, a month having elapsed, Madame Villard was again preparing to motor through the coun-

A UNIQUE OLD WINDMILL IN PICTURESQUE FRANCE

try to search. She intended to stop at a little graveyard in the Argonne (är-gŏn′) and pray.

And while Madame Villard waited thus for little Jeanne, Suzanne Moreau was bringing the baby to Paris.

On the tramp Suzanne had found the child a sweet and tender thing. Little Jeanne had hardly ever cried. She was satisfied and sleepy, or gurgling and gay.

Her life had been a rough one and her feedings irregular and sometimes insufficient. Still the baby had seemed happy, and Suzanne had smiled a great deal more than she had ever before smiled in her life.

Before the march was over, little

Jeanne was the only child Suzanne had ever kissed.

For a long time after reaching Paris, Suzanne Moreau's only thought was to tend this baby for whom she had promised to care.

She expected to take the baby to the home where it belonged. But her first thought was to give the child a few days' good care and food before giving her up.

It was a thought which Suzanne would never have admitted was selfish. But the truth was that little Jeanne's baby fingers had so tenderly wound themselves about the heart of Suzanne Moreau that already the thought of parting with her was unbearable. A few days passed. Then a week, and then more days.

"I should. I should," sighed Suzanne, as she watched the little girl sucking contentedly on her bottle.

Then when the bottle was emptied, Baby Jeanne lifted her two pink hands.

In her arms Suzanne rocked the baby back and forth and murmured, "No, no, my little one, ma chérie (mä shĕr-ē′, which means "my dear" in French), I cannot give you up. Not yet."

This went on for some time. At last one night Suzanne determined to go to that address on the Avenue Champs Elysées. She went alone. She left the child in the care of a woman with whom she boarded.

Before the tall stone building, Suzanne stood and marveled. It seemed a palace to the little village dressmaker. How could she keep this child from a home like that? To-morrow, yes, to-morrow, she would take Jeanne to her rightful home.

As she turned to leave, a big motor car drew up at the curb, and a black figure stepped out. Madame Villard had returned from another unsuccessful search. She was returning to her daughter and to little Margot, discouraged, disappointed, and heartsick.

Little did she know that the slight figure turning the corner was Suzanne Moreau. Little did she dream that this

THE MARIE ANTOINETTE COTTAGE NEAR VERSAILLES
PALACE

woman turning the corner was hurrying back to her own grandchild, who slept in a poor little Paris boarding house.

Suzanne began to arrange the few little clothes she had bought for Jeanne. She made a bundle. Then she took from her drawer the locket which the child had worn about her neck. She opened it.

Paul's face seemed to be smiling at her. Often before she had opened this locket, but never had the soldier face seemed so happy as now. Suzanne knew why. It was because she was going to take Jeanne to her place—her rightful home.

Her heart was fluttering and her

hands were shaking as she put the
locket about the child's neck. Then she
sat by the little cradle. Before she
knew it, the tears were falling down
her cheeks.

Why did she care this way? Suzanne
asked herself. She had lived alone for
many years. For many years she had
had nothing to love. Why could she
not go on?

Why must this tiny bit of life, sleeping so sweetly before her, make all this
difference and make her cry?

Jeanne stirred. The little pink hands
went up. It was a gesture Suzanne had
come to love, to wait for, to thrill at.
Slowly she raised Jeanne from the cradle and held her.

The baby's hands gently touched her cheeks. One little hand was patting a wet, wet cheek.

Then it stopped, and a soft head slowly sank upon Suzanne's breast. Jeanne was asleep.

Suzanne sat staring ahead of her. The baby had made a decision for Suzanne.

Cruelly and unfairly, in her mind Suzanne blamed little Jeanne for the decision she made that night. But her torn heart could not have stood the blame. She knew and felt only one thing.

To the sleeping child she cried, "I cannot, cannot give you up, my little Jeanne. Never, never!"

The locket with the soldier's picture was put away under lock and key. And Madame Villard continued to wait for her grandchild.

CHAPTER VI

JEANNE

Jeanne grew under the loving and tender care of Suzanne. Never once did Suzanne approach the stately apartment house on the Avenue Champs Elysées. Never once did she allow Jeanne to go in that direction.

Several years passed. Jeanne was now a tall girl. But still Auntie Sue had a terrible feeling about that apartment house.

Suzanne was still known as Auntie Sue. And between the poor little dressmaker and Jeanne, Auntie Sue's Shop had grown up in Paris.

JEANNE

Paris, you know, is the place from which your mother's or auntie's or grandmother's most fashionable clothes come. Nearly everyone who visits Paris buys a Parisian gown.

The French are well dressed. The French dressmakers know well how to cut and fit and sew.

Then, too, when little ones go to Paris with their mothers, they, too, are fitted with dresses and hats and coats made by the Parisian dressmakers.

Auntie Sue fitted many, many children. She fitted children who lived in Paris, also children who came from America and Spain and Italy and Germany and from other parts of the world.

For Auntie Sue's Shop was well
known. It was known because, for one
thing, Auntie Sue was clever and could
make beautiful children's clothes.

It was known for another reason, and
perhaps a better one. That reason was
Jeanne!

Jeanne put on all of Auntie's little
models. She showed them to the people who came to buy clothes for their
children.

Jeanne walked about the pretty little room, with its dainty show-cases
and Parisian dolls and model coats and
hats. She walked about the room and
wore the clothes that Auntie Sue had
made.

And when the children's mothers

THE WINDOW OF AUNTIE SUE'S SHOP IN PARIS

came to buy, they said, "Isn't that a beautiful little coat?" or, "Doesn't she look sweet in that little dress?"

Jeanne always looked sweet and pretty in everything she wore. Jeanne walked very straight and held her head high and smiled at all the people. She seemed to belong in those clothes.

So every mother thought that her child would look as well as Jeanne looked. Of course some of them did, but not all. Jeanne was known throughout Paris—throughout "child-and-mother-Paris" — as the "Little Model."

You may think that she became haughty and proud because so many people knew about her and came to watch her. But this was not the case at all.

Jeanne never thought of things like that. She was too busy ever to think of such things. While she loved to help Auntie Sue, it was hard work, and often Auntie Sue worried.

"Ma chérie," she would say to Jeanne as she stroked her silky brown curls, "you are happy; are you not? You do not mind the work—the hard, hard work? Ah, Jeanne, it is not pleasant sometimes, I know."

And this was true. For when many, many mothers and children came, Jeanne had to walk back and forth, back and forth, through the room. She had to show the silken dresses, the velvet coats, the little fluffy bonnets and hats. And she always had to smile and answer people's questions to the tune of that smile.

Then when changing behind the screen in Auntie's tiny dressing room, she had to be careful with the clothes —very careful. If lace should tear or a frock become soiled, Auntie would not be able to sell it. It was a careful little girl who changed behind that screen.

But Jeanne would always answer Auntie as she smiled into her worried eyes, "No, no, dear Auntie Sue. Never am I sad. Never do I mind the work. It is play, you know. All the other little children envy me!"

This also was true. Many children did think what fun it would be to wear all those lovely clothes and step about that gay little shop.

Some even went home and tried to imitate Jeanne. They thought it was fun. They did not know it was hard, hard work.

Jeanne answered Auntie Sue this way and really meant what she said.

Still Jeanne often wished for the days to be much longer. Jeanne wanted to play.

It was all right for those other children to play at being Jeanne. But really to be Jeanne was not play!

When those other children wearied of their game of being Jeanne they

SHE HAD TO BE CAREFUL WITH THE CLOTHES

stopped. Jeanne could never stop. And there was never any time left for her to play.

Auntie Sue often noticed that Jeanne's eyes held a wistful look. Auntie Sue mistook that wistfulness and thought Jeanne was longing to possess the beautiful clothes she showed.

She thought that Jeanne was sad because, each day, she would have to take off those lovely clothes and put on her own simple little dresses.

It was only natural for Auntie to suppose this because Jeanne loved and caressed each new garment that Auntie made. She seemed always so happy to put them on.

But here is a secret: Jeanne never once thought about those clothes after she took them off. She liked her little gingham dresses just as well.

In fact, Jeanne would not have cared one bit what she wore, if only she could have played. Auntie Sue did not know that.

CHAPTER VII

MAJOR d'ARTROT

One morning Major d'Artrot (där-
trō) received a letter from an old
friend. It was a good friend: Madame
Villard. Madame Villard wrote that
she expected to spend a night at the
Major's inn.

A tiny tumbled farm was Major
d'Artrot's Inn. Before the war it had
been his fine and prosperous home. But
the Major had been obliged to turn his
home into a hotel. For the war had
made him a poor man.

Fighting and scenes of horror had
taken place on that peaceful farm. It

had been occupied by the Germans. Later a terrible battle, one of the famous battles of the Argonne, had been fought there.

In the Major's garden stands the "Bloody Tree." The name is enough to tell what happened beneath its

THE BLOODY TREE

tall branches. A pole with wires still stands outside the Major's house. It is a telegraph pole raised by the Amer-

ican soldiers during the war. When
the war was over, people came to see
the Major's farm. People were curious, interested. There was the cellar
where some poor souls had lived for
weeks, listening to the booming of the
battles in the woods near-by.

There were the German helmets cap-
tured during that last battle. There
were many, many reasons why travel-
ers were drawn to Major d'Artrot's
farm. So Major d'Artrot turned his
house into a hotel. One of his dearest
friends was Madame Villard. She had
helped make life easier for the Major
and for his little brood.

During the long years following the
death of her son, the Major had tried

to help the stricken mother in her search for her lost granddaughter.

He had at last gathered for her the information that on that fa- mous march an old peasant had been seen with a baby. Some one had seen him. But he had fallen on

AMERICAN TELEGRAPH WIRES IN THE MAJOR'S GARDEN

the weary march. They knew that.

But they did not know about the ba- by. Nobody could tell Madame Villard what had happened to the baby.

To-day the Major received Madame Villard's letter.

"Poor Madame!" he sighed, as he finished reading. "She does not give up hope, even through all these years."

And he thought of the little black figure which soon would step from the big, glossy car. She would take what comfort this poor family could provide. She would make happy the Major's children with gifts and toys. Her simple room would be generously paid for.

Then Madame would leave them, and to the near-by cemetery she would go. She would visit it, before starting the journey homeward to Paris and to her little Margot. Usually these visits of Madame Villard occurred after a tour of the country. Those tours took her into very many villages of France, and always for the same purpose—always for a possible sign, a tiny clue of her lost grandchild.

"Madame is here," called the Major's youngest. "The big bright car is outside. See! Madame is coming in."

A flock of eager youngsters gathered about the little lady. She kissed them all and then sat down in the coolness of the Major's hallway.

"I have traveled far," she told the Major, after they were settled comfortably. The Major's children were outside in their arbor opening wonderful packages.

The Major's children were not starved for play. True, Madame Vil-

MAJOR D'ARTROT AND HIS FAMILY

lard was the only one who gave them shop toys. But their playthings were the brooks of the forest, the little farm animals, and sticks and stones.

Happy little d'Artrots! The Major did not worry because they were so poor. They had plenty of time for play.

"Through Verdun (vĕr-dŭn´) and Reims (rēmz) and the valley of the Meuse (mūz) I have traveled, dear Major d'Artrot," said Madame Villard. "My travels have now become a habit. There is surely no more hope. But on and on I go."

Major d'Artrot took her hand. "You must not say that, dear Madame," he answered. "There is always hope. And remember what joy you bring with your visits to us. We are always so glad to see you."

Madame thanked the Major and smiled.

"You are kind," she said. "I am always happy here with you and with your little dear ones. But this time my visit is to be short. I must leave for Paris to-morrow."

"So soon? That is a pity," the Major said.

"No," smiled Madame Villard. "My little Margot's birthday is coming soon. I have promised to return and see to a very important part of her celebration."

Madame Villard's eyes were now twinkling. "Can you guess what that very important part might be for a young miss and her birthday?"

"No, I am afraid I do not know," the Major said.

"Well, dear Major, the young miss is to have a party frock which Grand-

REIMS CATHEDRAL

mother will give her. Now do you admit that is a most important part of any young lady's birthday celebration?"

"Yes," laughed Major d'Artrot, "very important and serious!"

Then Major d'Artrot pulled a little card out of his pocket and showed it to Madame.

"And since Mademoiselle (mȧd-mwȧ-zĕl') Margot is to have a beautiful frock," he said, "why do you not take her to this old friend of mine who makes some of the loveliest frocks in Paris?"

Madame Villard read the card and then looked up at the Major questioningly.

VERDUN

He continued, "Suzanne Moreau lived in the village adjoining my farm before that village was destroyed by the enemy. She was a demure little dressmaker, and we knew her, my wife and I, as a kindly and lonely soul. Now

THE MEUSE

as you see by this card, she has estab-
lished a fashionable children's shop in
your Paris. She is still a kindly, modest
little woman. Her whole life is cen-
tered in that small niece of hers,
Jeanne, who is called the 'Little Model.'
Have you, perhaps, heard of her?"

Madame Villard nodded and looked again at the card.

"Auntie Sue's Shop," she read.

"Yes, indeed," she answered. "I have heard. But Margot and I have never been to the shop. Now since I know that they are friends of yours, we will surely go."

"Ah, you are kind," said the Major. "Auntie Sue deserves what little one can do to help. She is struggling alone and works very hard. I assure you, dear Madame Villard, that she is a most deserving and honest person."

"I believe that," smiled Madame, patting the Major's hand. "For to be a friend of yours, one is obliged to be deserving, honest, and kind."

CHAPTER VIII

THE GUIGNOL

Auntie Sue watched Jeanne as she skipped along to school. There could not possibly have been a happier skip. There could not possibly have been a happier little face than the one Auntie Sue had just kissed.

But yet as Jeanne turned the corner, Auntie Sue felt something sad inside of her.

Something said to her, "She is not really happy. Other children are happy, but Jeanne is not a child. She is a puppet—a puppet."

Suzanne rushed into the shop and

tried to shut out those thoughts. And Jeanne skipped along to school.

Strange to say, Jeanne was thinking of puppets, too. But she was not thinking of them in the same way as was Auntie Sue.

She was thinking of the puppet show in the park. This puppet show is called a Guignol (gēn'-yōl) in France and the park where it is played is the Champs Elysées.

On nearly every corner of this beautiful park is a Guignol. Where there is no Guignol, there is a swing, or there are donkeys to ride or goat carts. Children are amused in Paris.

Jeanne often passed the park, but the amusements there were not for her.

THE GUIGNOL

Jeanne had no time for Guignols and donkeys and goat carts. Jeanne had to go to school and from school to help Auntie in the shop.

The donkeys and swings and other amusements did not attract Jeanne so much. But oh, how she loved the Guignol! Very often she would stop outside the tall gates and watch for ever so short a time.

And when the children cried out, "There he is! There he is!" as they do when the wicked policeman pops up his puppet head, Jeanne would shout with them.

She loved those silly little puppets. She knew them all just by passing them each day.

There was Guignol, the bad boy. He
was the one all the children loved.
There was the policeman; and how
they hated him! There was a funny
lady with a wobbly hat, which was always knocked off; and her hair would
all fall down.

There were others. There was a pale,
very pale boy they called Pierrot
(pyĕ-rō′) which, in French, means
"clown."

Jeanne felt sorry for him because he
was very old and paintless and torn.
They never gave him a fresh coat of
paint nor mended his suit. Poor Pierrot!

Jeanne knew those stories by heart,
too. There was the story of the milk-

man. The bad boy drinks all the milk-
man's milk, while sending him on use-
less errands.

There was "The Mattress," the story
in which Guignol has a dream right up
on the tiny stage. Guignol, by the way,
is just like our American Punch, a puppet of the Punch and Judy show.

There were a few other stories, but
they were always the same. Jeanne
thought of many new stories. She wondered why the children didn't grow
tired of having the same stories all the
time. Jeanne could make up others—
and she did—while she skipped to
school. She made them up while
she walked about the shop showing
Auntie's little models.

To-day was a very fine day. When school was over, Jeanne found a group of children in bright-colored clothes, watching the Guignol. How sweet and pretty they looked sitting under the trees in their dainty clothes!

Jeanne leaned against a tree. It was early yet. She might watch one Guignol play.

The play was "The Thief." Guignol gives a lady a rose. She puts it in her hair under the large, floppy hat.

Then Guignol dances for her. It is a clumsy dance, and he trips. The children laugh. He gallops clumsily off the stage. Pierrot tiptoes in from the other side.

Jeanne leans forward eagerly. Has

JEANNE LEANED AGAINST A TREE

Pierrot a new suit, new paint? No, he
is shabby and pale. Ah, poor Pierrot!
But he dances on tiptoes, so light is he.

His dance is elfin and gay. The lady
watches. She is enchanted. Pierrot flits
about the stage. Then, when his dance
is at an end, he snatches the rose from
the lady's hair. The lady's wobbly hat
falls off. The lady's wobbly hair falls
down. She is a sorry sight.

But who is that entering on the side?
It is Guignol! He marches up to Pierrot, and there is a fight. The children
scream. The children cry out. Pierrot
is losing.

"Ah, Guignol! Guignol!" the children
cry.

Their hero is winning.

Pierrot is thrown, and he lands far away from the stage. He lands on the ground, but the children do not mind.

They are all absorbed in Guignol—their Guignol. He is kissing the lady now.

But not for long are they happy. The alligator comes gliding upon the stage. There is another battle, and Guignol vanquishes the alligator.

Then indeed is Guignol a hero. The curtain falls to the pleased applause of the young audience.

Only Jeanne has noticed Pierrot. He lies in a heap on the ground. Nobody has come to fetch him.

Time goes on, and as the sun sinks lower, more and more children leave

the park. The Guignol plays are over
for the day. The men who make them
are packing to go.

Now everyone is gone but Jeanne.
Jeanne and the Pierrot are alone. The
little girl goes up to the puppet.

"They have forgotten you, Pierrot,"
she says softly, "but maybe they do
not care."

Then Jeanne sits down on a bench
with Pierrot in her arms.

"But come, come. You must not
mind, Pierrot, if they do not love you.
You must not mind if they throw you
aside and clap for Guignol. See! I love
you very much. And even if you do
wear shabby clothes and your paint is
dull, that does not matter."

Jeanne rocks the Pierrot. It grows dark in the Champs Elysées.

"You must not mind. See, Pierrot!" she says. "See my dress and coat and cap? They are as shabby as yours. But I do not mind. You see, we are both the same. But I feel sorry because you do not dance more and because you are never the hero of the plays. Guignol is an awkward, clumsy fellow. It is you who are my hero, Pierrot."

As she talks, Jeanne's voice grows soft and drowsy. Jeanne's head nods, and her eyes close. A soft breeze begins to stir in the trees. Jeanne is asleep.

CHAPTER IX

AN ADVENTURE IN THE BOIS

Jeanne and Pierrot were walking through the Bois de Boulogne (bwä′ dē bōō′-lōn′). That is a beautiful wood in Paris where children and grown people play and walk and go boating on silvery lakes.

Jeanne and Pierrot walked in the Bois (bwä), hand in hand. Pierrot was not crying any more, though it had taken Jeanne a long time to soothe him. She told him of the many stories she would make up. She told him of the many fine adventures he would have as the hero of these stories.

90

Jeanne now had a story in her mind. And she was taking Pierrot to a quiet spot where she could tell him about it.

"Sit here beside me, Pierrot," she said at last.

They had found a sylvan dell that might have been in the heart of fairyland, instead of in the heart of a big city like Paris.

"Now, listen, Pierrot," said Jeanne. "I am going to tell you a very fine story. You and I shall be the actors in it. I shall be Joan of Arc and you shall be my knight.

"You know that Joan of Arc was only a little girl when she heard the call to save her country. She rode a big horse at the head of an army.

THE BOIS DE BOULOGNE

"She marched against the enemy with a sword in her hand. But my story says that without her brave knight she could not have won the battle."

Pierrot's shirt puffed out. His little clown cap went up in the air—puff!—and came down again on his head. He was very proud indeed. Jeanne was pleased because she had made him happy.

"Now see! We shall begin our story and I am hearing the call."

Jeanne stood; but first she picked up a long stick from the ground. The stick turned into a sword—a glittering sword.

Jeanne was dressed in shining steel armor. Pierrot's tiny clown suit changed to a coat of mail. They were ready for the battle.

"Forward, my brave men of France," called Joan of Arc. And the little puppet saluted Jeanne. But Jeanne cried, "My horse! Where is my horse?"

A large statue appeared before them. It was the iron statue of a horse. It was twice the size of a real horse.

Jeanne tried to mount. She could not. She was too small. The horse was too high. But Pierrot mounted. With a graceful leap, he was upon the charger's back. Then down he flew and offered Jeanne his hand. Up flew the puppet, and Jeanne flew with him.

They sat upon the iron charger. Slowly he moved his joints, and then

off, off he galloped with the little girl
and the puppet.

All the time Jeanne was brandishing
her sword. She was Joan of Arc and
she was riding at the head of her army
of France as Joan of Arc had done
long, long ago.

"Wait, wait!" called a voice. A policeman was running after them
through the Bois. "Stop! You have
stolen a statue from the park. Bring
back the iron horse!"

He was so little—that policeman—
and the horse was so big that they did
not mind him.

"He is only a policeman," said Jeanne
to Pierrot. "He is always clubbed and
kicked in the Guignol plays."

Pierrot laughed, and pop!—part of his armor burst!

"Oh, he is a wicked, wicked policeman," said Jeanne. "The children always hate him in the Guignol plays."

So away from the policeman they galloped.

But wait! Look! The policeman has grown, and he is now as tall as the horse! The club he carries has grown, too, and he clubs the iron horse. It makes a terrible noise, and the horse stops.

Knock! Knock! Knock!

"Wake up, little one!" says a gruff voice.

Jeanne opens her eyes and looks into the face of a policeman standing over her in the park. She has been asleep on the bench, with the little puppet Pierrot in her arms.

It is very dark in the park. It is night.

"Come," says the policeman. "Tell me where you live, little one."

Oh, the terrible policeman of the Guignol plays! Jeanne remembers how the children hate him, and she tries to run away.

But the policeman catches hold of her arm. It seems to Jeanne that his face is kind.

"Come, little one! Do not be afraid of me. I am the friend of the children. Tell me where you live and let me take you home," he says.

It was very dark in the park, but as

they walked through the city streets, the lights made everything as bright as day.

Jeanne and the policeman and Pierrot came to the door of Auntie Sue's Shop. When the policeman handed Jeanne to Auntie Sue, the little girl could not help wondering why the children hate the policeman in the Guignol plays.

"Oh, Jeanne, my little one, ma chérie! Where have you been?" cried Auntie Sue.

It was quite evident that poor Auntie Sue had been worried ill. She caught the little dreamer and the puppet into her arms. She hugged them so tightly that Jeanne thought they would both

be crushed. Jeanne was more con-
cerned about Pierrot than about herself, though, for he was so little and
frail.

Then Auntie put Jeanne to bed with
Pierrot beside her, his face peering out
from the covers.

And when Auntie had left them
alone, Jeanne whispered to her little
puppet friend, "Pierrot, the policeman
shall not be bad in our stories! He is
good, you see. In our stories you shall
be the hero. The policeman shall be a
kind man who loves children. Guignol
shall be the wicked one, and you shall
kick and beat him."

Pierrot did not move. Jeanne was
awake now, you see. And puppets do

not move by themselves when children are awake.

But Jeanne thought she saw his eyes twinkle and his nose wriggle just the least bit, before she popped off to sleep.

CHAPTER X

THE LIVE PUPPET

After Auntie left Jeanne and the Pierrot asleep in bed that night, she went into her own room and sat down by her little table. She shaded her eyes with her hands and thought very hard.

Poor Auntie Sue was unhappy. There was a little voice inside of her that never would be still. This voice talked and talked and talked. No one could hear it but Auntie Sue. It was not a person, nor was it a fairy. Yet it was there, and it talked to Auntie Sue.

People call that voice Conscience. You see, many other people beside

Auntie Sue have heard that voice. He
is known to everyone who does wrong.

And Auntie Sue had done great
wrong. Not knowing it, she had been
doing a great wrong all these years she
had kept Jeanne from her rightful
home. And now that voice called Conscience was tormenting her.

To-night he was talking more loudly
and more fiercely than he had ever
talked before. As Auntie Sue sat before her little table, he did not leave
her a moment's peace.

"You see what has happened," he
said inside of Auntie Sue. "You see
what you have done by keeping Jeanne
from Madame Villard. She is starved
for play.

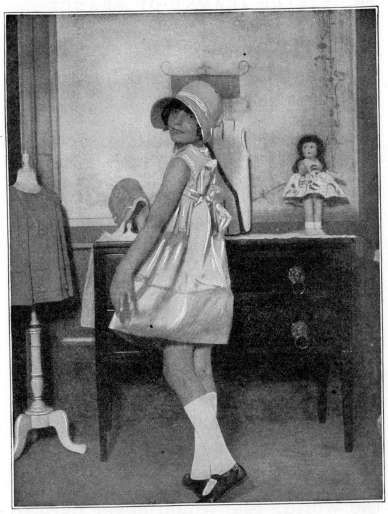

JEANNE SHOWING A NEW FROCK

"You have made her a poor little girl who has to work. If she lived in the lovely apartment house with her grandmother, she could play and play and play."

Suzanne clapped her hands over her ears to stop the voice. But Conscience. came from her heart and did not need her ears to hear him.

He went right on, "What would that soldier say? What would the old man say? What would the grandmother say? And Major d'Artrot?"

"Oh, Major d'Artrot, my good, my honest friend!" sobbed Suzanne.

She thought of her only friend in all the world. She would never dare to confess to him what she had done!

She opened her drawer and looked at the picture in the locket. She read again the name and address which had been pinned to the baby's skirt so many years ago: "Madame Villard. Avenue Champs Elysées."

The face of Jeanne's father looked back at her. It seemed to her that his eyes were accusing her.

"You have kept her from her rightful home and from the pleasures of childhood," went on the voice. And the face in the locket seemed to agree with the voice.

"To-night the child stayed in the park with a puppet—the only play toy she has ever had. She fell asleep in front of the Guignol, where happy children

SHE READ AGAIN THE NAME AND ADDRESS

go to clap and laugh. But you give Jeanne no time for play and laughter."

It was all true. But Suzanne knew that if Jeanne stopped showing the clothes she made, her audience would cease to be interested. If she did not draw her audience, she could not sell the clothes. And if she did not sell the clothes, she could not support Jeanne.

It was all quite terrible for Auntie Sue. And she dared not mention it to a soul. Nobody knew that Jeanne did not belong to her. Nobody knew Jeanne's story, not even the Major.

CHAPTER XI

LITTLE SPOILED MARGOT

"Grandmother! Grandmother! Home again! How glad I am!"

Little Margot threw herself into Madame Villard's arms, and the old lady hugged her close.

"Yes, my little Margot. Grandmother comes back for one splendid occasion!"

"Ah, my birthday," smiled Margot.

And then Grandmother and Margot planned for that birthday. It was strange how Margot did not like so many things.

When Grandmother mentioned a

108

theater party, the little girl shook her dark head.

"No, it is not what I like," she said.

Then Grandmother suggested a trip to the zoo with a party of girls and boys.

"No, I do not like the zoo!" Margot pouted.

"A Guignol party, chérie?" asked Grandmother.

"Ah, no! They are so stupid!" complained Margot.

And Grandmother smiled and shook her head.

"My Margot is a little bit spoiled, perhaps," she observed.

Margot was not a little bit, but a great big bit spoiled. Grandmother and Mother had both spoiled her, from the day she was born.

Mother was nearly always with Father and Margot saw little of her. When they were together Mother would kiss and hug a great deal and sometimes she would cry. There were always gifts in Mother's room for Margot.

And when Mother brought her into Father's room, he, too, would pet and caress her and give her toys or candy. Poor, helpless Father! He loved to see his little girl. It made his dull eyes brighten when she came into the room.

He would say to Mother after Margot had left, "Has the sun gone under a cloud, Marie? It seems darker to me."

You see, he felt sunshine while his little daughter was there.

But the nurse would not allow frequent visits. Ah, Father might never be allowed to forget that bitter war!

So Grandmother played guardian to Margot. And a loving and indulgent guardian was she!

Margot could play from morning until night if she wanted to, except, of course, for school hours.

The nursery was filled with costly toys. They did not interest little Margot any more. There were so many of them.

In fact, little spoiled Margot was not interested in anything, because she had too much.

"Ah, well, chérie," said Grandmother, "you will think of something that Grandmother can do for your birthday. But to-morrow we shall go to buy the little party frock which I promised you."

Frocks were of no more interest to Margot than toys. She had too many of those, also. So she hardly listened to Grandmother's last remark.

"I am going to take you to a shop where a little girl shows clothes to the people who come to buy—a real little model . You might call her a live puppet. My chérie will enjoy that, will she not?" asked Grandmother eagerly, hoping to interest the child in a new pleasure.

Evidently the idea did bring with it something new and exciting to Margot.

For she turned and asked, "And does this little girl really walk about and pose, as people do on the stage?"

"Yes, chérie. So I hear," answered Madame Villard.

"A live puppet!"

Margot clapped her hands, and Grandmother was pleased to see her joy.

Then her face fell, she turned to Grandmother and said slowly, "Oh, what a lucky little girl she is!"

CHAPTER XII

AT AUNTIE SUE'S SHOP

"The people are waiting! Hurry,
Jeanne!" called Auntie to the little girl
at the back of the screen.

Jeanne sat with Pierrot before her,
and both were dressed in splendor. The
little girl had on a new frock of Auntie
Sue's.

Her dark hair made a charming
frame for her little oval face under the
yellow poke bonnet, of old-fashioned
shape.   She wore an old-fashioned
dress.   It was yellow, with hand-
painted flowers and a velvet bow.

And Pierrot! Ah, Pierrot, too, was

fine in a new satin suit and cap, with bright red cheeks which Jeanne had painted. Many exciting adventures were happening there behind the screen to the little yellow-gowned girl and the clown in satin.

Jeanne was not thinking of this new frock of Auntie's which she wore, nor of the big Saturday audience out in the shop waiting for her to appear. She was thinking of her latest play for Pierrot. As Auntie called, Jeanne put the puppet down and, smoothing the dainty dress, she stepped out into the bright little shop room.

All about were seated ladies and children. The children were in smart attire, with interested and curious little faces that peered and stared at the live puppet as she walked about.

As Jeanne passed a little girl with hair and eyes as dark as her own and a wistful look, the gray-haired lady sitting beside the little girl stopped Jeanne.

"What a beautiful frock!" she said, and touched the hem of the garment gently.

Jeanne and the little girl looked at each other.

Auntie Sue came over to them.

Madame Villard smiled at the dressmaker and asked, "Do you think that this style would become my little granddaughter?"

Suzanne looked quickly at Margot.

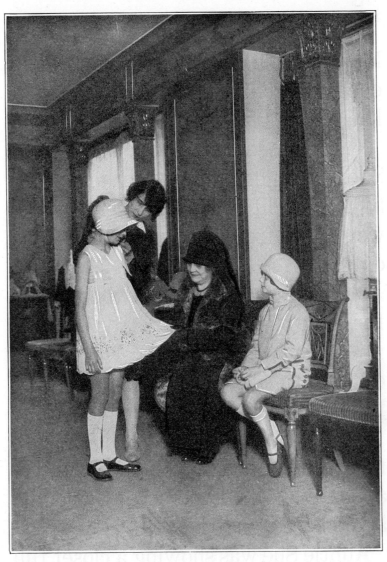

"WHAT A BEAUTIFUL FROCK!" SHE SAID

Margot's big brown eyes were fastened eagerly upon the child whom she had called a lucky little girl.

"Yes, Madame," answered Auntie Sue. "With her brown eyes and slight figure, the little mademoiselle should wear the frock as well as Jeanne does."

Madame and Auntie Sue then talked for some time about the frock.

Jeanne went about the large audience, with Margot's wondering eyes following her every movement.

At last Jeanne finished showing all the garments. The young model disappeared behind the screen, and the audience began to leave.

Auntie Sue was showing a closet full

of clothes to Madame Villard whose many purchases made the pencil of Auntie Sue skip over the page and her heart skip with gladness.

This was, of course, dull for Margot, and Margot was not used to things being dull. She sat in the empty room, while Grandmother talked and looked at clothes and paid no attention to her.

The little girl began to walk about the shop. She peered at the floppy dolls on the tables and at the quaint hat stands and show-cases.

She came to the screen behind which Jeanne had disappeared. She longed to peep behind that screen. She edged up close and tried to look through the cracks to the back.

She heard a tiny sound. Then words: "Down with the Bastille (bås-tēl´)!"

Margot pressed her head against the screen to hear better. The screen began to topple. Over it went. There was a muffled sound, and Jeanne stood up and faced Margot.

Jeanne was now in her own simple clothes. She held the Pierrot puppet, who was, however, still grandly dressed.

She stared hard at Margot and then at the fallen screen. Margot stared, too. Then Margot managed to remember her manners.

"Excuse me," she said. "I did not mean to knock down the screen."

Jeanne smiled and picked up the

screen, while Margot helped her set it in place. When it again stood erect, Margot found herself outside and Jeanne inside. They were separated as before.

For a few moments there was silence from both sides of the screen. Then came a giggle from one side and a giggle from the other.

And then from the outside, "May I come back and see you?"

From the inside, "Yes, do come!"

Margot went behind the screen, and for the first time in her life she learned the magic of real play.

Jeanne had one plaything: a little forsaken puppet. But with love and tenderness she made him a hero.

Jeanne told Margot about Pierrot. She told that he was no longer the buffoon—the poor mistreated clown. He was now a hero.

He could play a knight or a king—Napoleon! She told Margot that Pierrot was Napoleon in one of her plays and that she was Joan of Arc.

Margot lived in another world for the space of an hour. Then the two little girls were called back suddenly by a voice from the room.

"Margot, Margot! Child! Where are you?"

Grandmother was looking for her.

Margot and Jeanne stepped out from behind the screen and found Grandmother preparing to leave. Auntie

Sue stood beside her with pencil and pad.

"Thank you, Madame," said Auntie Sue gratefully, "for your splendid order to-day. It was indeed kind of you to make so many purchases at my little shop."

Madame answered, "I am truly pleased with your charming wares, my dear Mademoiselle Moreau. Besides, you know, my dear friend Major d'Artrot is also a friend of yours."

"But Madame," said Auntie Sue, as the grandmother and her little Margot started out of the door, "I have not yet taken your name. I do not know—."

"Of course, of course," laughed Madame Villard. "How very forgetful of me! Please write my name and address, so you will know where to send the little things."

Suzanne seated herself at a tiny desk and, with pencil poised, looked up at the sweet face above her.

Madame dictated: "Madame Paul Villard. Avenue Champs Elysées."

The pencil dropped from Auntie Sue's hand. Her head fell forward. Jeanne rushed over to the little desk and caught Auntie Sue as she was about to fall.

"Auntie, Auntie dear, what is the matter?" she cried.

Little Margot picked up the pencil while both children and Madame Villard hovered over the desk.

"IT IS ALL RIGHT. I AM ALL RIGHT NOW—"

Suzanne rested her head on her hand and whispered, "It is all right. I am all right now. I was only a bit faint. Oh, I am so sorry, dear Madame."

Auntie Sue was soon up upon her sprightly little feet again. Smilingly she bowed Madame and her granddaughter out of the door. But when they had left the shop, Suzanne went to her room, and Jeanne did not see her again that day.

CHAPTER XIII

COME AND PLAY

Margot took off the telephone receiver and asked for a number. It was early next morning, and the child was not yet dressed.

She was in kimono and slippers and had tiptoed into the living room.

"Hello," said a voice at the other end of the wire.

"Hello," said Margot. "I want to speak with Jeanne, if you please."

Margot had talked of nothing but Jeanne from the time she had left the shop. She had fallen asleep last night to the tune of Pierrot dreams, fiery steeds, and gallant armored knights.

Grandmother promised that she might ask Jeanne to play with her to-day. They would go for a long drive. They would go to the park and to the Guignol. There was nobody like Jeanne —nobody that Margot had ever met.

"Is this Jeanne?" asked Margot, as the little girl's voice came over the telephone.

"Yes."

"This is Margot. Can you go out with me to-day? I shall call for you at two."

It was a command, but little Margot was not aware of that. She did not mean it that way. She only meant to have what she wanted, as she usually did.

"But I must first ask Auntie," Jeanne replied.

"Oh, she will let you go," declared Margot. "You may tell her that we shall take care of you and bring you back safely."

Margot waited while Jeanne ran to Auntie's room. Jeanne had not seen Auntie since the afternoon before, when she had so mysteriously disappeared in her room after her fainting spell. Jeanne found Auntie a pale and worried Auntie this morning.

"Oh, Auntie dear," cried Jeanne, throwing her arms about Suzanne's neck, "you are not well."

Suzanne assured the child that she was quite well, and so she was. The

THE LOUVRE—THE LARGEST MUSEUM IN THE WORLD

was quite well, and so she was. The

only trouble was with the little man who is nothing but a voice and is called Conscience. He had been talking to her all night and keeping her awake.

When Jeanne told what Madame Villard's grandchild wanted, it seemed that Suzanne flinched at the name.

But she smiled and answered, "Yes, dear. Tell her you will go. It will be so nice for you. And to-day is Sunday. There is no work."

Jeanne was only a child, and she longed to go with her new little friend. She longed to ride in the big motor and to play. But she hesitated just for a minute.

"You are sure you will not need me, dear Auntie?" she asked.

"Run along and tell the little girl you are coming," laughed Auntie Sue.

When Jeanne closed the door behind her, Suzanne Moreau's smile faded. She held her throbbing head in her two hands.

How she longed to tell some one of her sufferings! If only she dared confide her story to the Major!

But she valued that honorable gentleman's friendship so much that she feared to lose it by admitting what she now felt to be her terrible crime. Conscience was making her think that— Conscience, together with the face in the locket!

And now Jeanne was going out with little Margot—her own cousin! Mar-

THEY PASSED THE PLACE DE LA CONCORDE

got would take her in a beautiful car. Margot would wear beautiful clothes. They would play with beautiful toys.

Ah, poor little Jeanne! It was hard for Suzanne, with these thoughts, to keep a smiling face until Jeanne had left with Margot.

CHAPTER XIV

A DRIVE THROUGH PARIS

Through Paris in a fine motor car! How often Jeanne had seen these same sights! But now how splendid it all seemed to the little girl, as she sat beside Margot, with Pierrot firmly clasped in her hand! For Pierrot had been invited, too. I doubt whether Margot would have welcomed Jeanne as heartily without Pierrot. Pierrot was half of the performance.

They rode through Paris. They passed the Place de la Concorde (pläs dĕ lä kôn-kôrd′), that most beautiful of city squares, where a sight not so beautiful once stood. It was here that the guillotine had stood. It is the terrible instrument which beheaded so many people in those frightful, stormy days of old.

The square was then called Place de la Revolution (pläs dĕ lä rĕv-ō-lū'-syōn). But now the name, "Place de la Concorde," means "Place of Peace."

They crossed bridges. There are thirty-two bridges in Paris. Some of these are very beautiful. Curiously, the oldest of these, a bridge begun in 1578, is called Pont Neuf (pôn nûf), which means "New Bridge."

They passed the Louvre (lōō'vr'), once a palace. It is now the largest museum in the world. Here such famous

THE ARC DE TRIOMPHE

works of art as the Venus de Milo (vē'-
nus dĕ mē'- lō) and the Mona Lisa
(mō' nä lē'-zä) are to be seen.

The Arc de Triomphe (ärk dĕ trē'-
ônf') stands as a memorial to the great
victories of the French general, Napoleon I. It is an arch of splendor set in
the center of branching wide avenues.

For Paris is a city noted for beauty.
It was planned and built and dreamed,
while most other cities, like Topsy, the
colored girl, "just growed."

Paris, with its avenues lined with
trees, its wide streets and spacious
parks, did not "just grow." It was a
dream before it was built, and now it
is that dream realized.

The little girls passed the spot where

the Bastille once stood. This was the famous prison into which people were thrown by the French kings, usually without fair trial. But one day the Parisians marched against the Bastille and burned it to the ground.

The little girls passed the Tuileries (twēl-rē′), which are fairy-like gardens. They are a children's paradise, and part of the dream that Paris is.

Margot and Jeanne watched the people sitting outside of cafés on the streets. They watched the fashionable strollers along the boulevards.

For Paris is well dressed, both inside and out. French cooking is an art, as is everything that these art-loving people attempt.

THE SPOT WHERE ONCE STOOD THE BASTILLE

At the end of their happy day the little girls drove to the park. They sat upon a bench beneath shady trees and they watched a Guignol play.

They had chatted and laughed and now were the very best of friends. Margot was a happy little girl that day. She had learned from Jeanne how to play.

"Sit still, Pierrot," scolded Jeanne softly so that only Margot might hear.

"Pierrot, you shall never come again if you do not behave!" continued Jeanne.

Margot was laughing, for she could see Pierrot bouncing up and down on the bench. Of course the other children couldn't see it, but Jeanne told Margot about it. So she could see plainly what this naughty puppet was doing.

"Oh, dear!" whispered Jeanne to Margot. "He will do something dreadful when Guignol comes on the stage. You know he cannot bear Guignol!"

There now was an ugly, red-nosed clown in the play. He had taken Pierrot's place after that day when poor Pierrot had been abandoned.

"Here comes Guignol!" exclaimed Margot.

Guignol slid upon the stage and fell flop!—on his nose. Guignol began to dance. But again he tripped over his big feet and landed puff!—on his stomach.

He stood up, grunting and groan-

THE TUILERIES—FAIRYLIKE GARDENS AND CHILDREN'S PARADISE

ing and puffing, and again he danced.

Margot and Jeanne watched Pierrot bouncing up and down. Jeanne had to catch Pierrot's hat each time it flew off, as it did whenever Guignol fell down on the stage.

Pierrot's hair stood up like wire, and the cap went up in the air. At least, that is what Jeanne said it did!

When the fight came, they could not hold Pierrot. He kicked and squirmed and waved his arms.

Jeanne was so shocked when his cap flew off and hit a gentleman in the eye! Margot was embarrassed, too. They scolded and spanked Pierrot, but it did no good.

"He wants to be in the play," whispered Jeanne. "I have spoiled him by making him the hero, and now he cannot watch Guignol!"

The children were relieved when at last the play was over. They were then able to take the unruly puppet away and bundle him into the car.

"My child always disgraces me! But we cannot blame him," said Jeanne, shaking her head like a fond but troubled mother. "He was so abused before, and now he has discovered what a great actor he is, and what a hero!"

"Oh, but Pierrot is splendid!" answered Margot.

And pop!—went a button on Pierrot's suit. His chest puffed out, and his hat flew off. The children laughed.

JEANNE AND MARGOT PLAYED IN THE CHAMPS ELYSÉES

When Margot left Jeanne at the door of Auntie Sue's Shop, she wanted to know when they should be together again. She asked when they should play more of Jeanne's stories with Pierrot.

Jeanne did not tell Margot that she would not be able to play again for many days. Work would interfere. Work was always there to stop play.

But Jeanne did not say this to Margot. Margot would not have understood. Jeanne only told her that she hoped they would meet soon again.

So with her puppet in her arms, she stepped out of the car. She stepped out of the car and out of a different world from her own.

And Margot planned all the way home to repeat to-day's pleasures to-morrow and to-morrow and to-morrow. Little, spoiled Margot!

CHAPTER XV
JEANNE AND MARGOT

Margot's to-morrow and again to-morrow with Jeanne did not come to pass.

Margot discovered she could not disturb the little girl's workaday life. It greatly annoyed Margot that, for the first time in her life, she could not wave her wand and command what she wished.

"I want her! I want to play with her!" exclaimed the pouting Margot, stamping her foot.

She had just called Jeanne on the telephone. Jeanne had told her that it

148

"COME, JEANNE, WE SHALL SEE THE GUIGNOL TOGETHER"

would be impossible to go to the Guignol or play.

To-day was a week day, and from school Jeanne was obliged to hurry home to help Auntie Sue in the shop.

"Come, Margot, child," pleaded

Grandmother. "Do not fret. We shall take another child to-day. Grandmother will telephone for you."

"They are all stupid! I want Jeanne!" insisted the little girl.

So Margot went to the Guignol with her nurse. She went again and again. All the time, she thought of the happy day she had spent there with Jeanne and Pierrot.

While Margot was watching the puppets one day, she noticed a child standing outside the gate looking in. It was Jeanne.

Jeanne was coming home from school and, as she often did, was watching Guignol's antics for a few brief moments.

Margot jumped up and, to the aston-
ishment of her nurse, she ran over to
Jeanne.

"Jeanne, how happy I am to see you!
Come in. Come! We shall see the
Guignol together," she cried.

But Jeanne shook her head, and her
eyes were sad.

"I should like to, Margot," she answered. "But Auntie is waiting. I
must go."

They stood there together for sever-
al moments. During those moments,
Margot caught once more the spell of
Jeanne's play magic.

For Jeanne played always. She
played while she talked or dressed or
walked. And while she watched the

Guignol, her playing was always splendid. Margot caught the spell.

Long after Jeanne had left she sat and played her own dream plays, while the play of the Guignol went on in front of her. Often after that day, Margot saw Jeanne hurrying home. But Jeanne never stopped again.

Jeanne often saw Margot after that day, but she hardly turned her head toward the park. She kept hurrying on because she was afraid of the tears that lived just behind her eyes when she passed the Guignol.

Those tears might at any moment break through the doors of her eyes. And Margot must not see that!

As Margot watched Jeanne, she wondered whether, after all, the little puppet was such a lucky little girl. She began to think of a really lucky little girl whose name was Margot!

One day when Margot came home, she said to Grandmother, "Grandmother dear, I have at last thought what you may give me on my birthday."

Grandmother took her hand.

"I am glad, chérie," she answered, "because the day is drawing near."

"If I may take Jeanne with me to the Bois and spend the day there, that is all I wish," said Margot.

"And no party?" Grandmother looked surprised.

"No. I prefer that," said Margot.

Grandmother telephoned to Auntie Sue. It was arranged that Jeanne was to be spared for that one day—Margot's birthday.

A day in the woods was planned with a picnic and a boat ride, but, best of all, with Jeanne and Pierrot.

The morning of Margot's birthday arrived. As the little girl opened her eyes, a dismal sight met them.

The gray sky was pouring down bucketsful of rain. The morning was as gray and dark as a rainy morning can be. Margot saw her day in the woods spoiled, and she started to cry.

But Grandmother arranged that Jeanne was to come to the apartment.

Margot's pout did not make of her a

very happy looking birthday girl. But she had to be satisfied with these plans.

"It would have been so nice to play in the Bois," she sulked.

"Yes, chérie," said Grandmother, "but we cannot change the weather."

And so in front of a crackling fire in Margot's toy stuffed nursery, the two little girls spent the day.

Margot met Jeanne with, "Isn't it too bad?"

But Jeanne could find nothing to feel sorry about.

"Oh, what a beautiful fire!" she exclaimed.

And after a little while, Margot began to be glad that the day was rainy, because Jeanne was glad.

CHAPTER XVI

"I WANT TO PLAY"

Auntie Sue worked very hard. She now had several large orders to fill.

She was finishing Madame Villard's order to-day, and she hoped to bring the little dresses to the apartment that evening.

Jeanne was spending Margot's birthday at the Villard apartment. So Suzanne determined to deliver the dresses and fetch Jeanne when the day was over.

She worked steadily and tried to banish thoughts and voices inside of her. Since Madame Villard's visit to the

AMERICAN FLAGS FLYING BESIDE THE FRENCH

shop, Suzanne had not had a moment's
peace from Conscience.

It was only the thought that Jeanne
really loved to show the pretty clothes
that kept Suzanne the least bit happy.

She answered Conscience thus: "But
see how happy the child is when I give

her a new frock to show! She knows, too, that she is the envy of every child in Paris!"

And Conscience always replied, "Perhaps. But maybe she is telling you that. Maybe she is really like any other child who wants and needs to play!"

This was the thing that always caused Auntie Sue to shudder. If she had thought that Jeanne cared, she could never have gone on asking her to work. She hoped that Jeanne did not like to play and did not mind being different from other children.

Always this hope made Auntie Sue argue with the voice. You see, Auntie Sue tried to believe that Jeanne was glad to be a live puppet!

AMERICAN CEMETERY NEAR ROMAGNE

Two little girls played and chatted before a crackling fire. While they sat in Margot's cheerful, rosy room, they made journeys throughout the land of France.

Stories and stories and stories!

Once Pierrot was a soldier, and they played the Great War. Margot and Jeanne were nurses. Through battle-fields of France they took their fancies.

Margot had motored many times with Grandmother throughout the valley of the war. She had passed villages, gray and ruined. She had passed villages, new and shiny, with American flags flying beside the French.

She had passed American cemeteries, with thousands of little white crosses like snow upon the ground. There were brown crosses, too, and huge stone monuments to soldiers.

There was one monument built around a line of bayonets where a company of soldiers had been buried alive

HUGE STONE MONUMENT TO SOLDIERS

by an enemy bomb. Their bayonets still show above the ground.

She had seen great tanks along the roadside—barbed wire and trenches.

Through beautiful France the little girl had journeyed with Grandmother.

Through the famous wine country—
the lands of Burgundy (bûr'gŭn-dĭ),
Champagne (shăm-pān'), and Dijon
(dē-zhôn'), the city of churches, pal-
aces, and famous mustard they journeyed!

Along the road sat women knitting
or sorting and cleaning the cotton of
their mattresses. They were washing
in little outdoor water troughs along
the roadway.

The children made a play for every
part of France. They made one for
every French character they had ever
heard about. Jeanne could weave a
play about anything, and Margot could
not help saying, "What a pity you do
not have more time to play!"

SHE HAD SEEN GREAT TANKS ALONG THE ROADSIDE

At this moment the doorbell rang. Auntie Sue was ushered into the hall by the Villard maid. Auntie Sue had come to deliver her parcel and to fetch Jeanne.

"Madame Villard is not in," said the maid, "but the children are in the nursery. Would you like to go to them?"

Thus it happened that Auntie Sue arrived at the nursery door in time to hear the two little girls discussing a serious question.

Auntie Sue did not want to eavesdrop. She would not have listened to the children if she could have helped herself. But the fact of the matter was that Auntie Sue became rooted to the floor, and she could not move.

For the first thing she heard was Jeanne's voice saying, "Oh, Margot! I hate all those silly clothes! I hate being a model. I want to be just a little girl."

Jeanne's voice was bitter. Is it any wonder that Auntie Sue could not move from the spot on which she was

CHAMPAGNE VINEYARDS NEAR EPERNAY

standing? She grasped the door knob to keep herself from falling.

Then the conversation went on.

"Then why do you do it?" asked Margot's voice.

"Because," came Jeanne's, "I dare not tell Auntie. She works so hard and

takes such good care of me. You see, I
have no mother and father."

There was silence, and then Jeanne's
voice went on, "My papa was a soldier.
But Auntie does not know where he
fell."

Again silence and then Margot said,
"I think your aunt would let you play
if you would ask her to."

"No," Jeanne replied, "I would not
ask her. I must show the clothes. She
could not sell them if I did not show
them first."

There was a short silence and then
again came Jeanne's voice, "I just want
to be a little girl. I want to play!" The
last word ended in a sob.

For the next few moments Auntie

Sue did not hear anything. Indeed she hardly knew anything, so stunned and shocked was she.

Auntie Sue did not know how it was that she ever opened the door. She did not know how she ever came to leave that apartment.

It was fortunate that Madame Villard and Margot's mother were out. Children do not always notice things the way grown people do.

But Margot wondered, after Jeanne and her aunt had left, why Auntie Sue's eyes had been so big and frightened and why she had hardly said good-bye.

LITTLE JEANNE OF FRANCE

CHAPTER XVII

A CALL FOR HELP

Major d'Artrot called to his wife, "Come; see! A letter has arrived which calls me to Paris. I must leave at once."

Madame d'Artrot read the letter.

"Dear, dear Major d'Artrot," it said, "You are my only friend, and I must ask you to come to my aid. I am in trouble. I need help and I am ill. Please come to me.

Suzanne Moreau."

"Why, that is Auntie Sue," said Madame d'Artrot, a surprised note in her voice. "She has such a successful shop, I am told. What can be the matter?"

A DIJON MUSTARD SHOP

"That is what I shall find out soon," answered the Major. And he made hasty preparations to leave for Paris.

When Major d'Artrot returned to his farm two days later, he brought with him a little girl.

Jeanne was a very white-faced little girl.

Major d'Artrot said, "I have brought little Jeanne to be our guest until her aunt is better."

And all the little d'Artrots flocked about Jeanne and tried to make her feel at home.

It was all so strange to little Jeanne from the city. She had been taken away from Auntie—Auntie, who lay ill and needed her.

But the Major told her to come. He told her that Auntie wished her to come with him. If Auntie wished it, Jeanne must go. But otherwise she would never—could never—have left poor sick Auntie Sue.

AN OLD WOMAN CLEANING THE COTTON OF A MATTRESS

Once outside in the fresh, pure country air, Jeanne began to forget a little. With rabbits and dogs and cats about her and the merry chattering of the Major's children, she could not help it.

Jeanne's eyes were alive, and her

heart was gay. She was one of the little fairies of play, and that kind of
fairy cannot remain sad for long.

Besides, the Major's children had
games and playthings of which Jeanne
had never before heard. Even Pierrot
was excited. It was all Jeanne could
do to hold him from jumping into the
little stream.

Jeanne soon had the young d'Artrots
acquainted with Pierrot. Indeed, the
young d'Artrots fell quite in love with
sprightly Pierrot.

In the meantime the Major recounted
to his wife the happenings which had
befallen him in Paris.

"Poor woman!" he told Madame
d'Artrot, as he described Suzanne's

WASHING IN OUTDOOR WATER TROUGHS

plight. "She is ill because of the wrong she committed so many years ago. She could tell nobody about it.

"But she finally discovered that Jeanne was unhappy, and that was too much for her to bear. She realized then that she was being punished for her wrong. And so she decided that before it was too late she would confess!"

"So she told you this terrible story?" asked Madame d'Artrot.

"Yes, and asked me to see Madame Villard," replied the Major.

"And when will you break this news to Madame?" the Major's wife inquired.

"I have already done so," he answered quietly. "That is, I called upon Madame Villard before leaving Paris. I told her that I had traced her lost grandchild. I told her that I wished her to come to our home to-morrow. But I did not tell her any more."

"Ah, poor Madame Villard! How happy I am for her! What a joy this will

be for her!" sighed Madame d'Artrot.
The Major smiled and agreed with
his wife.

"And what
a joy for this
poor little
play-starved
child!" he
said, looking
out of the
window at
the happy
band of chil-
dren.

THIS WAS A SOLDIERS' BURYING
GROUND

They were
romping and
making the air ring with glad sounds.
The next morning Jeanne arose

early. Being on a farm was something
so different and thrilling to this child
of the city that every noise outside her
window seemed to call her.

She put on her little black apron and
went out into the brisk country air.

The farm animals greeted her, and
the little stream gurgled good morning. This was the most beautiful feeling that life had ever given Jeanne.

She skipped about the farm, seeing
and feeling and smelling country,
freshness, and morning. It was beautiful.

And then she thought of Auntie Sue.
Ah, poor Auntie Sue! If only she could
be here with Jeanne! If only they could
forget that shop and come to a place

like this! Why hadn't Auntie Sue ever told her about places like this?

As Jeanne's thoughts flew, her little feet flew, too. Soon she found herself walking along the country road. New wonders met her eyes and ears and nose with every step. Her sadness was nearly forgotten, until she stopped.

There, in front of Jeanne, were countless crosses—crosses of white, crosses of brown, all in rows.

Margot had told her about the soldiers' burying grounds in the Argonne and in other places of France. This was a soldiers' burying ground.

The little girl stood and wondered.

She wondered about her own soldier father.

Just then a big motor car stopped not far away. Jeanne watched a black-gowned lady and child step out. They carried flowers in their arms. They went to a little brown cross and they knelt.

The tears welled up in Jeanne's eyes. Ah, how she, too, needed to pray! How she needed a little brown cross to kneel to—to talk to!

Everything was making Jeanne cry. She was wondering again about Auntie Sue. How strangely Auntie had acted! And she had sent Jeanne away!

CHAPTER XVIII

MARGOT'S STORY

"Come. Tell me. Quick!" Madame Villard breezed into the Major's house with Margot following. They were both breathless, excited. "What have you found out, dear Major? Tell me."

Major d'Artrot bade the eager grandmother be seated and rest herself. Then he asked one of his own little girls to take Margot outside.

"We can't find the little girl," said the Major's eldest to Margot, when they were outside in the garden. "When we came out this morning she was gone."

"What little girl?" asked Margot.

"Why, Jeanne," said the Major's daughter. "That little girl from the city. Papa brought her here last night."

When Margot learned that it was Jeanne—Auntie Sue's Jeanne, "the little model"—she rushed into the house.

"Oh, Grandmother, Jeanne was here. But now she is gone," she cried.

The Major looked astonished.

Grandmother had been crying.

"What is that you say, my dear?" asked the Major. "She is gone?"

"Yes. The children cannot find her."

Then the Major left Grandmother and Margot alone, while he went out to search for Jeanne.

And Grandmother held Margot very

close, while she repeated the tale that the Major had just told her.

"And so, my dear little Margot," she added, "Jeanne is your own cousin."

Margot could not speak. Her heart was too full. She only hugged Grandmother like a little bear.

JEANNE WAS KNEELING BESIDE A CROOKED LITTLE BROWN CROSS

Then, more like a swift jack rabbit, she flew out of the house. She flew out in search of Jeanne, her own cousin.

All the d'Artrots were looking for Jeanne, but Margot came upon her first.

Jeanne was kneeling beside a crooked little brown cross. There were flowers on it.

Jeanne had made the crooked little brown cross herself, and she was praying. She had made it for her soldier daddy.

Margot came up behind Jeanne.

"What are you doing, Jeanne?" she asked.

Jeanne thought she had never before seen Margot's face this way. It seemed that Margot was about to cry, but not the usual Margot cry.

She was not acting spoiled. She was not commanding anything. She seemed so sweet and kind and sympathetic.

"I—I was praying," said Jeanne. "But what are you doing here, Margot?"

Margot sat down beside the little, black-aproned figure and took Jeanne's hand.

"I came to play with you, Jeanne," she said. "I came to tell you about a new play."

Jeanne could not understand it at all.

With head bent, she whispered, "But Margot dear, I have not brought Pierrot. We cannot play without Pierrot."

Margot answered, "We do not need

Pierrot for this play. You see there is only one heroine, and that is you."

Then Margot told a story to Jeanne —a curious story of a little baby who was kept away from her grandmother and her cousin. Yes; the baby was really kept for a number of years from a home of love and pro-

THEN MARGOT TOLD A STORY TO JEANNE

tection and made to work. She had very little time to play. She did not even

know her real name. How could she?
It had never been told to her.

She told Jeanne of another little girl
who lived in that home and had everything. The other little girl could have
played always but didn't know how.
She didn't know how to play until the
first little girl came and showed her
how.

Then Margot told about a kind man
who received a letter from a sick lady
telling what a terrible deed she had
done.

The lady begged the kind man to
take the little girl to his home in the
country and then to send for her
grandmother and little cousin.

So he did. And when the grandmother and little cousin arrived, they found that the child was Jeanne!

Jeanne started, and her eyes grew big and round.

Margot put her arm about Jeanne's shoulders. Just then they heard a step.

There was Grandmother Villard standing among a group of young d'Artrots. Grandmother left the group and came over to the two little girls.

She took Jeanne in her arms. She cried.

And then she said, "Jeanne, my little one! My own little grandchild!"

The d'Artrots left, and Jeanne and Margot and Grandmother sat together for a long time. They sat silently.

But suddenly Jeanne exclaimed, "Oh, poor Auntie Sue! I must go to her. I must go."

Grandmother held her back.

"No," she said. "Auntie Sue is all right, Jeanne. She only wants you to be happy."

"Ah, but how can poor Auntie Sue sell the dresses now, when I am not there to

SHE TOOK JEANNE IN HER ARMS

show them for her?" asked Jeanne.

"She will not have to sell dresses any more," said Grandmother. "Grandmother will ask Auntie Sue to live with us always, Jeanne, if—"

"If what, Grandmother?"

"If you want her to," continued Madame Villard.

"Oh, poor dear Auntie Sue!" cried Jeanne. "She has been kind and good to me. She could not help doing what she did. I love Auntie Sue, and I want her to live with us always and always!"

"You are a good little girl, Jeanne. Your father would have been proud of you," said Grandmother softly.

Then Grandmother continued, and her voice was husky, "You have been as brave a soldier as he, Jeanne."

Grandmother arose. The two little girls followed her to the white dotted graveyard. They knelt before one of the white slabs. Jeanne saw her own father's name in letters before her. She tried to pray and to keep her eyes on those words, "Paul Vil-

"LET US GO HOME NOW AND PLAY"

lard." But the letters ran together.

A little breeze seemed to be whispering over and over to her, "Jeanne

Villard, Jeanne Villard—that is your name."

Grandmother and Margot at last arose. Margot put her arm lovingly about Jeanne's shoulder.

"Come, Jeanne, little cousin," she said. "Let us go home now and play."

PRONOUNCING VOCABULARY

Arc de Triomphe . . . . ärk dĕ trē'-ônf'
Argonne . . . . är-gôn'
Bastille . . . . bȧs-tēl'
Bois . . . . bwä
Bois de Boulogne . . . . . bwä' dĕ bōō'-lōn'
Burgundy . . . . bûr'-gŭn-dĭ
Champagne . . . . shăm-pān'
Champs Elysées . . . . shän'zä-lē-zā'
D'Artrot . . . . ' . . . där-trō
Dijon . . . . dē-zhôn'
Guignol . . . . gēn'-yōl
Jeanne . . . . jēn
Louvre . . . . lōō'-vr'
Ma chérie . . . . mä shĕr-ē'
Mademoiselle . . . . mȧd-mwȧ-zĕl'
Margot . . . . mär'gō
Meuse . . . . mūz
Mona Lisa . . . . mō-nä lē'-zä
Moreau . . . . mō-rō'
Pierrot . . . . pye-rō'
Place de la Concorde . . . pläs dĕ lä kôn-kôrd'
Place de la Revolution . pläs dĕ lä rĕv-ō-lū'-syôn'
Pont Neuf . . . . pôn nŭf
Reims . . . . rēmz
Tuileries . . . . twēl-rē'
Venus de Milo . . . . vē'nus dĕ mē'-lō
Verdun . . . . vĕr-dŭn'
Villard . . . . vē-lär'